First published by Parragon in 2012
Parragon
Queen Street House
4 Queen Street
Bath BA1 1HE, UK
www.parragon.com

ISBN 978-1-4454-7678-0

Printed in China

Storybook Collection

Bath • New York • Singapore • Hong Kong • Cologne • Delhi
Melbourne • Amsterdam • Johannesburg • Shenzhen

Contents

Disney
Phineas and Ferb

The Easter Eggs-travaganza

Written by Scott Peterson
Based on the series created by Dan Povenmire & Jeff "Swampy" Marsh

"**W**ell, we're off to the antiques store for our annual Easter Sale-a-palooza," Phineas and Ferb's dad said as he waved goodbye to the boys and their friends. "If Candace helps out this morning, can I count on you two for the afternoon shift?" he asked his sons.

"Yes, yes you can," Phineas said.

"Good," Candace grumbled. "I'm not missing dinner with Jeremy because you are building some Easter-mobile!"

10

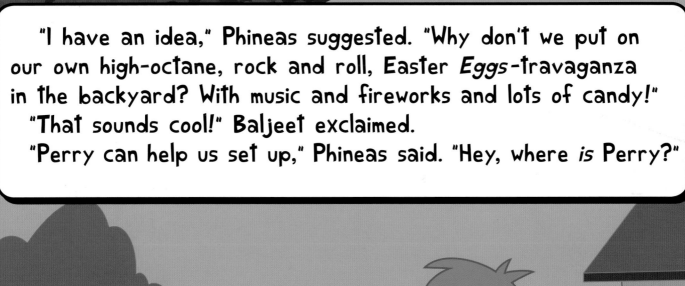

"I have an idea," Phineas suggested. "Why don't we put on our own high-octane, rock and roll, Easter *Eggs*-travaganza in the backyard? With music and fireworks and lots of candy!"

"That sounds cool!" Baljeet exclaimed.

"Perry can help us set up," Phineas said. "Hey, where *is* Perry?"

Perry the Platypus, now transformed into Agent P, had just arrived at Doofenshmirtz Evil, Incorporated to confront his number one enemy, Dr. Doofenshmirtz. The evil doctor was waiting for him. "Happy Easter, Perry!" he cried, pulling a lever. In an instant, the platypus was trapped in a giant Easter basket!

"Today, I have a *very* special scheme," Dr. Doofenshmirtz told Perry as he began to put on a bunny costume. "I've noticed that everyone seems to really *love* the Easter Bunny. You don't see that rabbit for 364 days of the year, but on *this* day, you welcome him with open arms. So now, *I* am going to dress like the Easter Bunny to gain access to City Hall and then take over the Tri-State Area!"

Meanwhile, Candace was at the antiques store, waiting for customers to arrive. She couldn't believe she had to spend Easter in a boring store when she could be doing a million better things! And she just knew that her brothers were up to... *something*.

Just then, Candace's phone beeped. It was a text from one of her friends.
"*Finally*, something exciting!" she exclaimed.

In Phineas and Ferb's backyard, the crazy Easter *Eggs*-travaganza was now in full swing! Jeremy and his band rocked the stage while everyone danced and cheered.

"In your *face*, Danville Easter Pageant!" Buford yelled, throwing his hands in the air.

A few minutes later, Isabella noticed two young kids who looked sad. They told her they were hoping for an appearance from the Easter Bunny.

"Phineas," Isabella began, "the kids are right. We can't have Easter without a bunny!"

"I agree," Phineas said. "And we don't want to disappoint the kids of Danville."

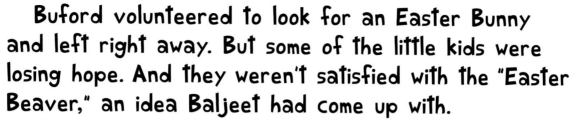

Buford volunteered to look for an Easter Bunny and left right away. But some of the little kids were losing hope. And they weren't satisfied with the "Easter Beaver," an idea Baljeet had come up with.

"I'm sorry, but we can't wait any longer," one of the kids' mums said. "We have to go."

"Just wait a few more minutes!" Isabella pleaded.

In the centre of town, Dr. Doofenshmirtz, now wearing a full bunny suit, was marching proudly towards City Hall. With Perry still trapped, there was nothing that could stop him now!

But what he *didn't* know was that Agent P was determined to escape from his trap. He was not about to let Dr. Doofenshmirtz ruin Easter for everyone!

The evil doctor had just reached City Hall when he was suddenly surrounded by kids! Some wanted eggs. Others wanted an autograph. One girl wanted to see him hop.

"I think I underestimated the demands of being a bunny on Easter," Dr. Doofenshmirtz groaned. Meanwhile, hiding in the shadows, Buford was ready to make his *own* demands of this bunny!

At the same time, Candace had just walked into her backyard and couldn't believe her eyes. The crowd. The noise. The weird guy on stilts. OMG! It was *totally* bustworthy! But then she spotted Jeremy onstage. Busting would have to wait!

Just then, Buford arrived backstage at the festival with the Easter Bunny he had found.

"Wait for your cue, fuzz ball. I'm going to get a snow cone."

"I'm trying to be a maniacal leader," Dr. Doofenshmirtz complained. "Not some lame kiddie entertainer. I'm out of here!" But before he could leave, Agent P dropped from the rafters to stop him!

"Perry the Platypus! You escaped *again*?"

As Dr. Doofenshmirtz and Perry fought behind the curtain, Phineas and Ferb took the stage to introduce a special guest.

Suddenly, Candace stormed up to them and held up her phone.

"If Jeremy's done playing, then *I'm* sending Mum a picture of you guys and this crazy festival!" she shouted.

"Ladies and gentlemen," Phineas announced, "give it up for our special guest - the Easter Bunny!" The cannon fired, spraying the crowd with confetti. The kids cheered as the bunny shot out of the cannon and flew over their heads!

Candace, startled by the loud boom of the cannon, stepped back and slipped. She was just snapping a picture to send to her mum when her phone went flying through the air!

At the antiques shop, Candace's mum had just received
a photo from her daughter's phone. It was a picture of
Dr. Doofenshmirtz dressed as the Easter Bunny.

"Well, it sure looks like Candace is having a good Easter,"
Mrs Flynn-Fletcher said to her husband. "But our store isn't. I
guess there's no reason to stay open without customers."

Phineas and Ferb's parents were closing up when Mr Fletcher spotted a crowd heading towards the store.

"We're following the flying Easter Bunny," Phineas told his dad, pointing to the roof. Dr. Doofenshmirtz had just landed there, still in his bunny costume.

"Then I guess we're still open," his father replied happily. "Come on in, everyone!"

As the crowd headed inside, Perry waddled up to Phineas and Ferb. He had put on an adorable pair of bunny ears.

"There you are, Perry," Phineas said. "Nice ears. Happy Easter!"

Phineas and Ferb

Thumbs Up!

Adapted by Lara Bergen

Based on the series created by Dan Povenmire & Jeff "Swampy" Marsh

It was another fun day of the summer holidays. Phineas and Ferb decided to tag along with their older sister, Candace, and hang out at the mall.

"All right, squirts," Candace said, handing Phineas some money. "I'm going to Mr Slushy Dawg."

Meanwhile, Perry the Platypus - also known as Agent P - was heading to his secret lair. He had a meeting with his superior officer, Major Monogram.

"Dr. Doofenshmirtz has purchased some suspicious items," Major Monogram told Agent P. "Four helicopter blades, two dozen party balloons and six thousand lightbulbs. Figure out what he's up to!"

Just then, Buford, the town bully, walked over. He sat down - right on Baljeet!

"Hey, Buford, that seat's taken," Phineas told him. Just then a scoop of ice cream fell off Phineas's ice cream cone - and right into Buford's lap!

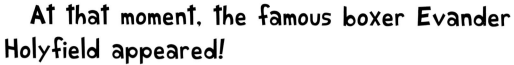

At that moment, the famous boxer Evander Holyfield appeared!

"If you have to fight, do it the time-honoured way: out behind the mall at three o'clock," he said.

Buford snarled. "Don't be late!" he told Phineas.

Phineas nodded. He was up to the challenge.

Phineas's friend Isabella gasped. She didn't want anyone to fight.

First, it was training time! Phineas knew he
had to be in tip-top shape to face Buford.
And he was ready to work as hard as he
could so he could defeat the town bully!

The boxer led Phineas through a series of exercises. First, Phineas warmed up by practising some fancy footwork.

Then, he ran up a flight of escalator stairs that were going down. Finally, he did a few sets of chin-ups on the jungle gym. Soon Phineas felt he was ready for the match.

Meanwhile, Candace had just heard about the fight. She headed outside and found Phineas and Ferb in the car park.

"You can't just go building a boxing ring out here," Candace told Phineas. "I'm telling Mum!"

Candace ran to the Squat N' Stitch. Her mum was onstage with her jazz band.

"Mum," she whispered, peeking her head through the curtain. "Phineas and Ferb are at it again!"

"Not now," Mrs Flynn replied. She was in the middle of playing a song.

Outside, the match was about to begin.

"Boys and girls - let's thumb wrestle!" an announcer called out.

At the sound of the bell, Phineas and Buford started to wrestle. The battle was on!

But no matter how hard Phineas tried, his
thumb was no match for Buford's.

Phineas slumped down in the corner of the ring.
"I don't think this is going so well," he said.

"Go for the gold!" Mr Holyfield urged him.

Across town, Agent P had found Dr. Doofenshmirtz at a cake factory... and found himself trapped in a giant bowl of purple batter! It was the evil doctor's birthday and he was baking himself a cake.

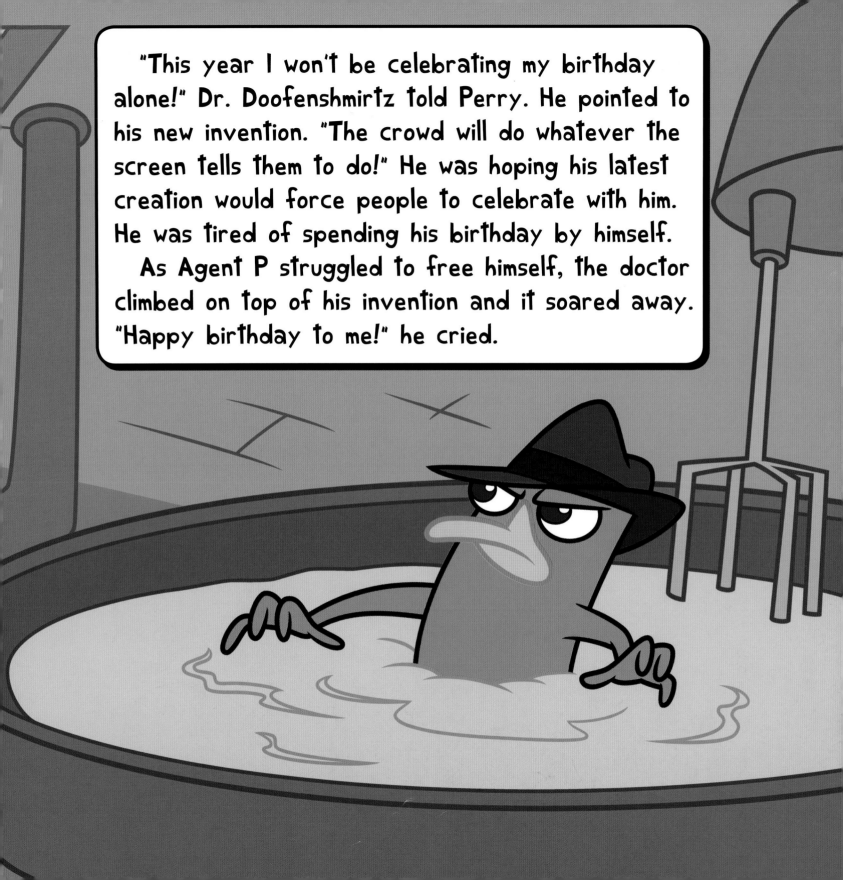

"This year I won't be celebrating my birthday alone!" Dr. Doofenshmirtz told Perry. He pointed to his new invention. "The crowd will do whatever the screen tells them to do!" He was hoping his latest creation would force people to celebrate with him. He was tired of spending his birthday by himself.

As Agent P struggled to free himself, the doctor climbed on top of his invention and it soared away. "Happy birthday to me!" he cried.

Luckily, Agent P had a plan. He pulled out a whistle to call for backup. Within seconds, a flock of bats flew into the factory. They ate every bit of cake mix. Soon Perry was free!

Dr. Doofenshmirtz was still flying on his invention, looking for a crowd of people. Just then, he spotted the audience watching the wrestling match below. It was the perfect time to launch his plot! But suddenly Agent P came zooming towards him!

"Look out for the party hat of doom!" the doctor yelled. He threw a pointy hat at Perry.

Agent P dodged the hat and then blew loudly on a whistle. In an instant, an enormous whale appeared! It knocked the ice cream cone that Dr. Doofenshmirtz was holding out of his hands. The scoop of ice cream fell towards the wrestling ring below.

In the ring, the thumb-wrestling match had just ended and Buford was crowned the winner. Suddenly, the ice cream that had fallen off Dr. Doofenshmirtz's cone landed right on Phineas's head!

"Ice cream fell on you!" Buford shouted, laughing. Now he and Phineas had both been embarrassed in public!

"What do you say? Even-steven?" Buford asked Phineas.

Phineas shook Buford's hand and smiled at him. "Sure," he replied.

As for Dr. Doofenshmirtz... he was no match for Agent P. The evil doctor was so surprised when he dropped his ice cream cone that he bumped into a giant pipe. His invention broke in two.

"This is the worst party ever!" Dr. Doofenshmirtz screamed. "Curse you, Perry the Platypus!"

But Perry was already on his way back home. His mission for the day was complete!

Just Squidding!

Written by Scott Peterson

Based on the series created by Dan Povenmire & Jeff "Swampy" Marsh

IT WAS ANOTHER SUNNY DAY of summer and the residents of Danville were very excited. Today was the opening day of the Danville Deep, the deepest body of water in the Tri-State Area! Phineas and Ferb were hard at work on a new project. Their friend Isabella walked up and looked at them curiously.

"We are building a super submersible mechanical squid!" Phineas told Isabella. He picked up his pet platypus, Perry. "We're going to go underwater and explore the lake. Just imagine what might be down there! Hidden treasure? Sunken ships? Old tyres? We might even find a whole new species of amphibious life!"

Further down the lake, Jeremy Johnson was ready to launch his rowboat into the water.

"Hey, Candace. Do you want to come fishing with me?" he asked.

"Oh, uh. I, uh, *fishing*?" Phineas and Ferb's older sister, Candace, stammered. Fishing was the last thing that she wanted to do! She would have preferred to go swimming or to just hang out with her friends. But she certainly wasn't going to turn down an invitation from Jeremy!

Jeremy rowed out to the centre of the lake. "This looks like a good spot to catch some fish," he said.

Candace smiled. "What a beautiful day," she said dreamily. Just then, she spotted Phineas and Ferb in their mechanical squid!

"What are my brothers up to now?!"

"Where are you going?" Candace yelled. "I'm telling Mum!" She grabbed the oars and began rowing towards the shore. But her mother was listening to music on her headphones and didn't hear Candace at all.

Meanwhile, beneath the surface, Phineas, Ferb, Isabella and Perry were just beginning their exploration of the Danville Deep. Giant, mechanical tentacles pushed them swiftly through the water.

"In addition to the tentacle propulsion," Phineas explained, "it's got turbo-fueled propellers, a rocket-powered escape pod *and* a full-service ice-cream bar!"

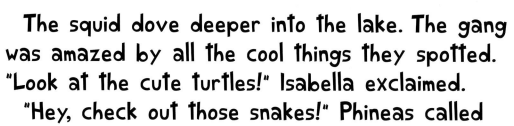

The squid dove deeper into the lake. The gang was amazed by all the cool things they spotted. "Look at the cute turtles!" Isabella exclaimed.

"Hey, check out those snakes!" Phineas called out. Then he looked around curiously. "Hey, where's Perry?" he asked. He had just noticed that his platypus wasn't there!

Perry the Platypus, aka Agent P, had just hopped into his own underwater vehicle. He was off on a very secret mission. Dr. Doofenshmirtz had built an underwater lair and Perry was determined to stop him from launching what was sure to be a new evil plot!

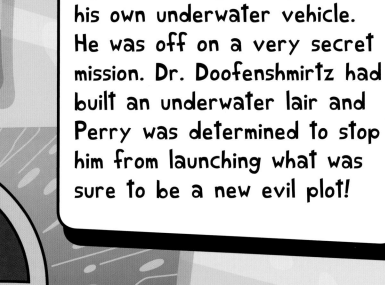

Agent P quickly put on his wet suit and charged into the lair. "Perry the Platypus?" Dr. Doofenshmirtz asked in surprise. "How did you know I was here?" He thought for a moment. "Oh, right. The big statue of me as King Neptune. I should really think these things through."

"Oh, well. Back to business!" the evil doctor announced. He unveiled his newest creation. "Behold!" he shouted. "My latest and greatest invention: the Aqua-Creature-Creator-inator! Or A.C.C.I., as the hip kids would say," he added.

"My invention hasn't worked perfectly yet," Dr. Doofenshmirtz admitted. "But this time, it is sure to succeed! How dare the citizens of Danville not invite me to opening day of the lake! With my invention, this tiny little fish will turn into a giant maritime monstrosity!" he yelled. "And I will defeat the Tri-State Area, once and for all!"

Dr. Doofenshmirtz pushed a button. The small fish suddenly transformed into a giant monster! Before Agent P could react, the doctor opened the tank. He shoved Perry and the monster into the waters of the Danville Deep!

The scary creature swam angrily towards Agent P, baring his very sharp teeth. He was quickly catching up to Perry!

As the monster lunged forwards, Agent P darted out of the way. The fish smashed into the lair, shattering its walls and blasting Dr. Doofenshmirtz with water!

"Curse you, Perry the Platypus," the doctor screamed as he quickly put on his scuba helmet.

Dr. Doofenshmirtz's creature swam around looking for Perry, who had used algae to disguise himself. Then the monster spotted the underwater vehicle and started heading towards it! But Phineas, Ferb and Isabella didn't see the massive fish. They were too busy checking out all of the cool things at the bottom of the lake!

"Buried treasure!" Isabella called out.

"An ancient submarine!" Phineas exclaimed.

"A vintage arcade game," Ferb reported.

"Mum!" Candace screamed. "Did you see? Phineas and Ferb brought that giant tree!"

But her mum's back was to the stage. "Candace, how could your brothers ever have moved a tree this big? I think maybe you've been out in the cold too long," she said.

Back on the mountain, Dr. Doofenshmirtz turned to reload his invention, only to find that Perry had destroyed it!

"Curse you, Perry the Platypus!" he howled, his angry voice setting off a huge avalanche that carried him away.

Perry snowboarded towards the party in Danville – Christmas mission accomplished!

Just then, the squid suddenly stopped.
"The controls are stuck!" Isabella cried.
"Let me see what's going on," Phineas said. "Oh! We're in the grip of... of, that!" he shouted, pointing to the giant fish.

The gang tried to manoeuvre their submarine's tentacles to pry it away from the monster. But Dr. Doofenshmirtz's creation wouldn't let go!

"What are we going to do?" Isabella asked.

"Wait. I think I understand what's going on here," Phineas said. "I don't think this giant fish is mean at all. He's lonely. And I think that it's made a new friend."

And Phineas was right. The creature was happily romping and playing with their mechanical squid!

"Well, that was exciting!" Phineas exclaimed. "I guess we should head back to shore now."

"But what about the treasures we found?" Isabella asked.

"We never said we wanted to *take* the treasures," Phineas told her. "We just wanted to find them!" The kids hopped into their escape pod and zoomed away. They left Dr. Doofenshmirtz's creation to swim with its new friend.

Just then, Phineas spotted his pet platypus. "Hey, there's Perry!" he exclaimed. "I wonder where he got those goggles from?"

Phineas, Ferb and Isabella quickly shot up to the lake's surface, right near where Candace and Jeremy were fishing. Candace was so surprised that she lost her balance and fell out of the rowboat! Jeremy, who was busy reeling in his fishing line, didn't even see Candace fall into the water.

"I got something! And it's a big one!"

Jeremy's catch was so big that he grabbed a fishing net to scoop it out of the water. His mouth dropped open in surprise. He had caught Candace! "Ooh, I'll get you next time, Phineas," Candace said, spitting out a mouthful of water.

Phineas and Ferb

The Best School Day Ever!

Written by Scott Peterson
Based on the series created by Dan Povenmire & Jeff "Swampy" Marsh

Phineas, Ferb and their friends stared at the television screen in awe. Boom! Crash! Pow! The stuntmen on TV were doing some amazing stunts!

That gave Phineas an idea. "Hey, everybody," he began to say, "I know what we're..."

"Yay, school!"

"Okay, guys," Phineas and Ferb's mum suddenly called out. "Your sister, Candace, and I are going to the mall. Your dad is taking a nap, so try not to make too much noise."

After his mum and sister left, Phineas turned to Ferb and grinned. "I know what we're gonna do today," Phineas said, finishing his thought. "We're going to build our very own stunt school!"

A few minutes later, the gang had changed into safety gear and got right to work. Buford carried equipment while Isabella lined the yard with safety cones.

Meanwhile, Baljeet was at his desk waiting for class to start. "I get the feeling that this is not the kind of school I was hoping for," he said sadly.

83

First up was a classic stunt: the human cannonball. Baljeet was very nervous giving this stunt a try. But Buford fired the cannon before he could say no.

A few seconds later, Baljeet shot out of the cannon and landed with a giant thump. "I'm a stuntman," he mumbled.

"This is awesome!"

For their next lesson, Phineas explained how to do cool trapeze stunts.
"I knew you'd flip for this," Phineas told Isabella.

Now it was time to learn how to leap across buildings. Isabella jumped across a row of makeshift rooftops and landed gracefully.

"Nice work, Isabella!" Phineas exclaimed. "You're a natural."

Perry the Platypus, also known as **Agent P**, had travelled to his secret headquarters to find out what evil plan **Dr. Doofenshmirtz** was plotting next.

But when he arrived, metal restraints snapped over his arms and trapped him! When he looked at the screen where Major Monogram usually appeared, he was shocked to see the face of Dr. Doofenshmirtz instead.

"Surprise!" Dr. Doofenshmirtz shouted. "I took over the spy agency with my newest invention: the Blow-'Em-Away-inator! I blew away some of the secret agents and locked them in a bathroom at Paul Bunyan's Pancake Haus! I've warned the other agents to not even *try* to come near me. Now I will be able to *finally* take over the Tri-State Area!"

Agent P was able to quickly break free from his restraints. But suddenly trash fell out of the ceiling and his own chair tried to attack him!

Dr. Doofenshmirtz laughed from the monitor. He was controlling everything in the lair to harm Agent P!

"Now you're in trouble!" the doctor cackled.

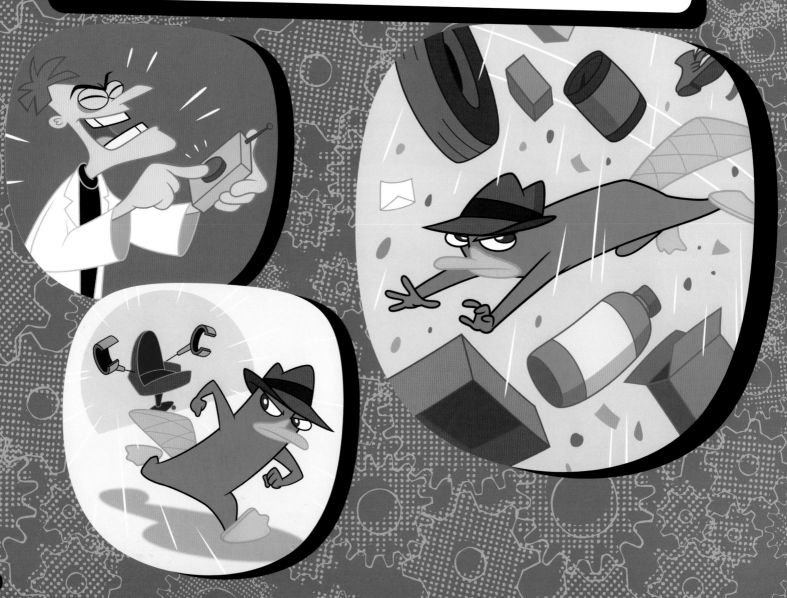

But Dr. Doofenshmirtz was no match for Perry. The platypus escaped from the lair, hopped in his hover car and sped away. The evil doctor climbed into his Blow-'Em-Away-inator and chased after him.

"All right, I'll follow you, Perry!" Dr. Doofenshmirtz shouted. "But once I blow you away, the Tri-State Area will be mine!"

Suddenly, Agent P heard a loud beeping. He looked down at his spy watch, where Major Monogram's face then appeared.

"Agent P, you've got to stay away from that -inator," he warned. "No one can recover from its high-powered winds... except maybe a stunt person."

Perry had an idea. He hoped it would work.

In the backyard, it was time for the stunt school final exam, an obstacle course full of challenges to test everyone's skills. Phineas explained that it would be difficult. But if they completed it, they would all be official stunt people!

Phineas started the course, with the rest of the gang following behind him. The first obstacle was triggered when a huge bucket of water overturned. The group skillfully jumped, flipped and dived out of the way.

Next, cardboard cutouts of angry ninjas popped up all around them! Isabella, Buford and Baljeet karate-kicked their opponents to the ground.

Up above, Agent P put his hover car into a dive and headed for the stunt course. Dr. Doofenshmirtz was flying right behind him.

"Come back here, Perry the Platypus!" he yelled.

"It sure is windy," Isabella commented, as powerful gusts blew through the course. Everyone managed to jump and leap out of the way. It was one of the toughest challenges yet!

"Why isn't my machine working?" Dr. Doofenshmirtz cried, as he noticed that everyone below was successfully dodging the winds from his -inator. Suddenly, Agent P jumped onto his back, causing the machine to spin and sputter. Then it started to blow the stunt school out of the backyard!

Agent P triggered his parachute and flew away. The-inator veered off in the other direction, dragging Dr. Doofenshmirtz along behind it.

"Curse you, Perry the Platypus!"

But Perry didn't hear the doctor yelling. He had already flown over to the pancake house to free Major Monogram and the other secret agents who were trapped.

"Good job, Agent P. Now, who wants an omelette?"

"Do we get our report cards now?"

The wind had finally died down in Phineas and Ferb's backyard. Everyone had managed to successfully complete the obstacle course!

"Wow, I don't remember programming a giant windstorm," Phineas said. "Do you, Ferb? Well, anyway, we did it!"

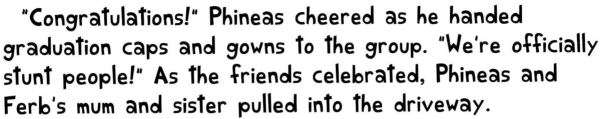

"Congratulations!" Phineas cheered as he handed graduation caps and gowns to the group. "We're officially stunt people!" As the friends celebrated, Phineas and Ferb's mum and sister pulled into the driveway.

"How cute," their mum said. "They're playing school." Knowing her brothers all too well, Candace did not think it was cute. They were definitely up to something!

"I'll get you next time, Phineas!"

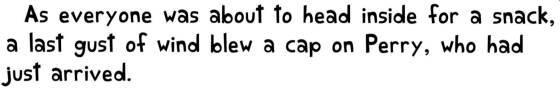

As everyone was about to head inside for a snack, a last gust of wind blew a cap on Perry, who had just arrived.

"Oh, there you are, Perry!" Phineas exclaimed. "Hey, you look good in a hat!"

Haunted Hayride

Written by Scott Peterson

Based on the series created by Dan Povenmire & Jeff "Swampy" Marsh

On a dark and spooky Halloween night, Isabella, Buford and Baljeet headed over to Phineas and Ferb's house. They couldn't wait to see what their friends had planned!

Phineas and Ferb had transformed their backyard into a spook-tacular sight. There were scary decorations, eerie music and even a giant corn maze!

"Awesome!" Isabella exclaimed. "But where are Phineas and Ferb?"

At that moment, Phineas popped up from behind a row of cornstalks. He was holding a crystal ball.

"Welcome," he said. "I predict a night of chilling surprises on our haunted hayride!"

Just then, Ferb drove up in a giant hay-filled wagon.

"Step right up!" Phineas announced.

   While Isabella, Baljeet and Buford climbed aboard,
Phineas and Ferb's older sister, Candace, poked her head
out of her bedroom window.
"Phineas! What's going on down there?" she yelled.
But no one could hear Candace shouting over the
tractor's loud engine.

"Ready for the best hayride ever?" Phineas asked, as they set off into the maze.

"Yes!" the gang cheered.

"Hey, where's Perry?" Phineas wondered, looking around for his pet platypus.

Perry the Platypus, aka Agent P, had very important business to attend to. He needed to get his orders from his superior officer, Major Monogram.

"Dr. Doofenshmirtz is planning on making this year's Halloween the scariest that Danville has ever seen," the major said. "You must put a stop to it!"

Moments later, Agent P crashed through a window into Dr. Doofenshmirtz's headquarters.

"Oh, hello, Perry the Playtpus," the evil doctor said with a cackle. "I've been expecting you."

All of a sudden, Dr. Doofenshmirtz trapped Agent P in a giant jack-o'-lantern! Then the doctor began to explain his latest plan.

"As a child, the older kids in my neighbourhood would always scare me on Halloween," he told Perry. "But tonight the tables have turned. I will be scaring everyone with my Rampaging-Monster-inator!"

Agent P had to act fast. He slyly escaped from the jack-o'-lantern and charged at the wicked doctor. Just then, Dr. Doofenshmirtz's creation was accidentally switched on! The robot burst through the wall and headed towards the centre of Danville.

Perry was determined to stop the runaway monster.
He flung a jack-o'-lantern over the evil doctor's head.
Then Agent P ran out of the building.

Back in the corn maze, the friends were having a blast.
"This is the coolest hayride ever!" Buford exclaimed.
"Woo-hoo!" Phineas cheered.

Meanwhile, Candace was desperate to bust her brothers. But as she wandered into the maze, she was getting very nervous. There were scary things everywhere!

All of a sudden, a giant spider leaped out at her. She fell backwards into a puddle.

"Phineas!" she snarled.

But Candace wasn't about to let a spider stop her from her mission. She was so determined to catch up to the hayride that she ignored a loud noise behind her.

Finally, Candace turned around.

"Aaaah! " she screamed. She started to run as soon as she saw the frightening monster.

Luckily, Candace quickly found her way out of the maze. She headed towards her friend Jeremy's house. He was having a party and her parents were going to be there, too. Candace had to tell them what she had just seen!

When Candace arrived at the party, she banged loudly on the front door.

"Mum!" she cried. "Guess what happened!"

Mrs Flynn looked at Candace and smiled. "I thought you were going to be Cleopatra for Halloween. But I like your zombie costume better," she said.

"But, but, but..." Candace stuttered.

In the maze, the friends were getting worried. The growling and crashing was growing closer and closer. "I-I-I think we should get out of here," Buford stammered.

Ferb drove faster and faster. The monster roared as it trampled cornstalks. Then the twisting maze led the group into a dead end!

"Fortunately, this is no ordinary hayride," Ferb told the group. He hit a button and lawnmower blades and rocket engines popped out of the bottom of the tractor!

"Hang on!" Phineas yelled.

The friends zipped through the corn maze. But the Rampaging-Monster-inator was quickly catching up to them! Ferb drove even faster.

"It's gaining on us, Ferb!" Phineas shouted.

Ferb nodded and hit another button. A pair of wings snapped out. The vehicle began to fly through the air!

As the monster continued its chase, Agent P appeared! He quickly jumped on top of it.

As the two struggled, the platypus noticed a dial on the creature that read **GO HOME**. He reached out and turned it.

The monster shot through the air. It headed right for Dr. Doofenshmirtz!

"Curse you, Perry the Platypus!" the evil doctor yelled. Agent P had defeated him - again!

Phineas and the gang had finally escaped the maze. Ferb parked the tractor and turned off the engine. "We made it," Phineas said with a sigh of relief. "But wait!" Isabella cried. She pointed at the rustling corn. "Something is still chasing us!"

As the cornstalks parted, out stepped... Perry!
"Hmm, I guess it was Perry that was chasing us,"
Phineas said. "He must have been trying to catch up
to the hayride all along. Who wants to go for another
hayride?"

Phineas and Ferb

Oh, Christmas Tree!

Written by Scott Peterson
Based on the series created by Dan Povenmire & Jeff "Swampy" Marsh

It was Christmas Eve, and Phineas and Ferb were waiting for the town celebration to begin. But the mayor had bad news.

"The annual lighting of the Christmas tree is cancelled. Our prize evergreen was destroyed in a freak accident," he said.

"Ferb!" Phineas exclaimed. "I know what we're going to do today. We're going to find the perfect tree!"

Phineas and Ferb's older sister, Candace, overheard her brother. "I have to find out what Phineas is up to," she thought.

Later on, Phineas and Ferb's friends stopped by.
"Whatcha doin'?" Isabella asked Phineas.
"Building a souped-up, rocket-powered, all-terrain,
evergreen-detecting supersleigh," Phineas told her.

Soon the sleigh was ready and the friends jumped inside.

"Everybody ready to go?" Phineas asked.

"Hey, where's Perry?" he asked, looking around.

Meanwhile, Perry the Platypus, aka Agent P, was heading into his secret lair. It was time to find out his assignment for the day.

"Hello, Agent P," Major Monogram, Perry's superior officer, said. "Dr. Doofenshmirtz is behind the destruction of Danville's Christmas tree. You must find out what he's up to!"

Phineas and the gang were about to leave when Candace burst into the backyard.

"Not so fast, you two," she said. But Phineas couldn't hear her over the loud engine as they started to speed away. Candace lost her balance and fell into a rubber ring attached to the sleigh!

The group travelled up into the mountains in search of the perfect tree. The sleigh changed into a snowmobile to climb the steep hills. Candace was trailing behind them, unnoticed.

Suddenly, the sleigh came to a screeching halt.
"Uh-oh. The trail is too narrow for the sleigh," Isabella said.
"We'll go on foot," Phineas told them.

"You sure it's safe to be out here all alone?" Buford asked.

"We're not alone," Isabella replied. "Phineas is here-"

Then, all of a sudden, a large, snarling yeti jumped out!

"Th-th-th-" Buford stammered. "That's the abdominal, abominomable-"

"Abominable snowman," Baljeet corrected him.

"Aaahh! " everyone screamed.

Meanwhile, at the top of the very same mountain,
Dr. Doofenshmirtz was preparing his latest evil invention.
Just then, Agent P sailed in on a hang glider!

The doctor quickly trapped Perry in a cage.
"Behold!" Dr. Doofenshmirtz cried. "My Snow-Hurl-inator! I am going to use it to make a fool of my brother Roger, the mayor, by hurling a giant snowball onto the town square!"

Down the mountain, the yeti was approaching. "Phineas, what are we going to do?" Isabella cried. "Don't worry," Phineas said. "He doesn't want to hurt us."

"Right," Ferb said in agreement. "Yetis are vegetarians. And they rarely show aggression unless they feel threatened."

Phineas turned to the yeti. "We only came for one special tree and we brought seeds to plant in its place," he said.

The yeti smiled. Soon the group was playing together like old friends. They played freeze tag, made snow angels and built snowmen.

Candace, however, was not having any fun. She had run into icy rocks, prickly thorns and hissing raccoons. "I'll get you, Phineas," she muttered.

It was time for Phineas and Ferb to get back to their mission.
"Hey, Mr Yeti," Phineas said, "where can we find a giant tree?"
The yeti pointed to a beautiful evergreen in the distance.
"That's it!" Phineas shouted.
The yeti yanked the giant tree from the ground. Isabella and Buford planted the seeds.
"Danville's celebration is going to be saved!" Phineas exclaimed.

Atop the mountain, Dr. Doofenshmirtz was about to fire his Snow-Hurl-inator into the centre of town.
Just then, Perry broke free and leaped at the doctor!

But Dr. Doofenshmirtz used his Snow-Hurl-inator to pummel the platypus with endless snowballs.

"In five more seconds, Danville's celebration will be ruined!" the doctor yelled.

Time was running out. Perry grabbed a snowball and threw it at the Snow-Hurl-inator. It hit the controls just as the invention fired. Then a gigantic snowball flew high into the sky... in the wrong direction!

Further down the hill, Candace saw her brothers in the distance. "They are so busted," she said, heading towards them. Just then, the massive snowball landed behind Candace and rolled after her!

The tumbling snowball picked up Candace as it rolled down the hill. It stopped near Phineas and the group, blocking their sleigh... and their view of Candace.

"Hop onto the tree, everyone!" Phineas shouted. He waved to the yeti. "Thanks for your help!"

At the last second, Candace jumped on the tree trunk and held on for dear life. Whoosh! The friends slid down the snow-covered mountain, riding the giant tree like a mighty bobsled.

As the tree sped into town, it picked up decorations and other things along the way. "We're almost there, everyone!" Phineas yelled. "Hooray!" the gang cheered.

Back in Danville, everyone was shocked to see a giant tree heading right for them. Thwack! The tree hit the edge of the stage and tossed the gang safely out into the crowd. The townsfolk cheered.